Oh. Hello.

You're probably wondering what I'm doing here in the dark.
By myself. With all this stuff.

If you guessed that I tried to run away tonight, you're right. I did.

Why? Well, that's a long story.

I can tell you, if you'd like.

My name is Louie, by the way.

Or it was. Now they just call me...

For Stacey and Kahlua

First published 2017 by Walker Books Ltd, 87 Vauxhall Walk, London SE11 5HJ • This book has been typeset in Myriad TiltBold • Printed in China •
British Library Cataloguing in Publication Data: a catalogue record for this book is available from the British Library • ISBN 978-1-4063-7671-5 • www.walker.co.uk • 10 9 8 7 6 5 4 3 2 1

Poor Louie

Tony Fucile

WALKER BOOKS
AND SUBSIDIARIES
LONDON • BOSTON • SYDNEY • AUCKLAND

My life was great!

Every morning started with a walk,

rain

or shine.

On Sundays we would do fun things,
like go for a stroll in the park,

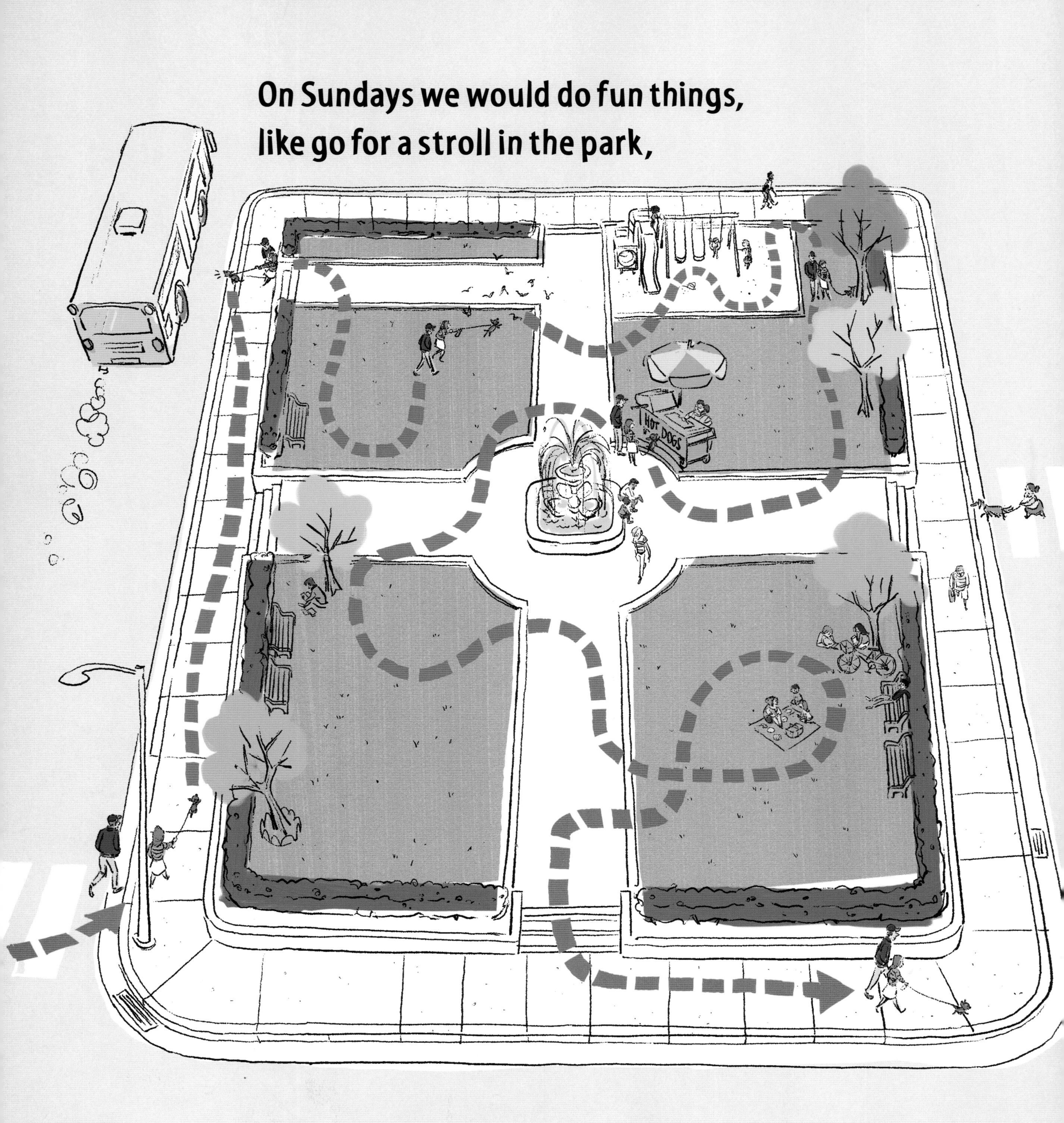

eat ice cream,

or go shopping.

Pretty much every day of the week ended the same way:

dinner,

a movie,

a kiss good night,

and then off we went to sleep.

Once in a while, Mum and I would
meet up with her friends.
It was great!
Everyone paid attention to me.

But then, one day, *they* started to appear.

First there was just one ...

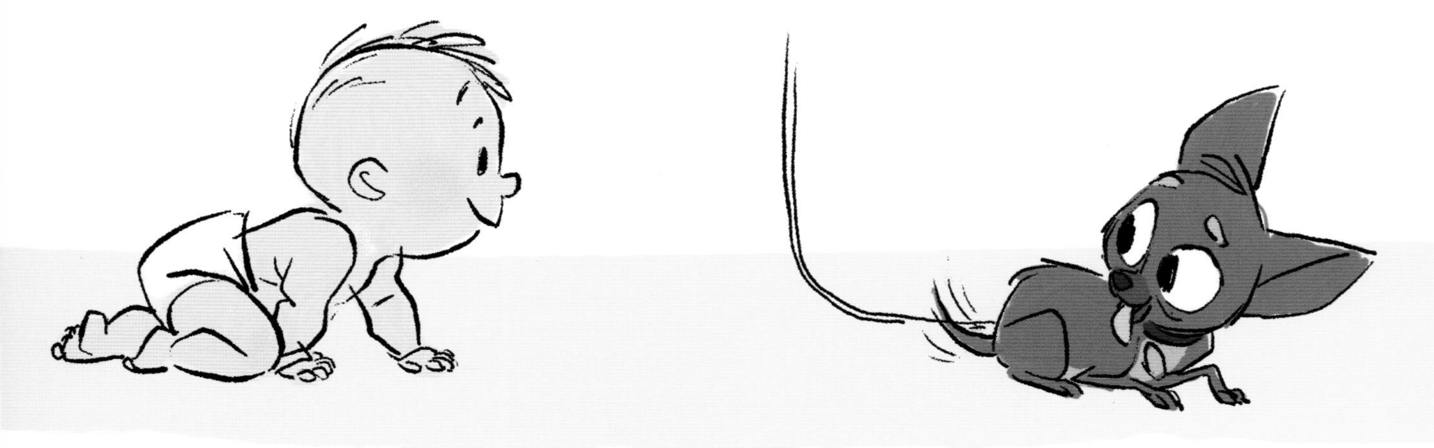

then two ...

then four...

They pulled on my ears

and squeezed my tummy.

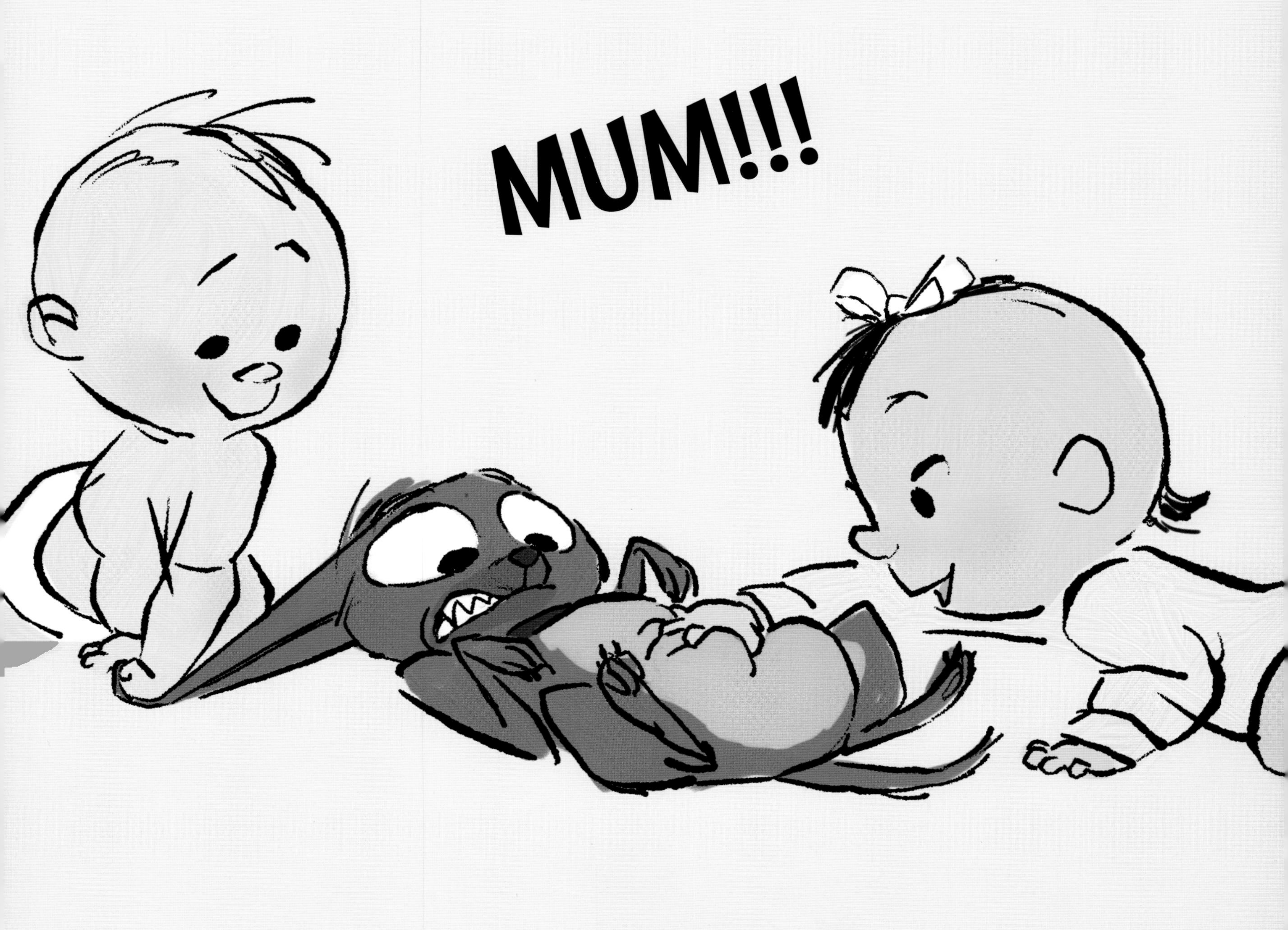

"Poor
Louie!"

Yeah, I know ... they smell good. And they do walk on all fours, I'll give them that. But YIKES! All I could say was thank goodness we'd never have one of those in OUR house.

Yep, life was pretty perfect with just the three of us.

Then, let me tell you – things got weird.

First it was dinner.
Cold.
On the floor!

I still had my walks, I guess.
Sort of.

Bedtime wasn't fun at all any more.

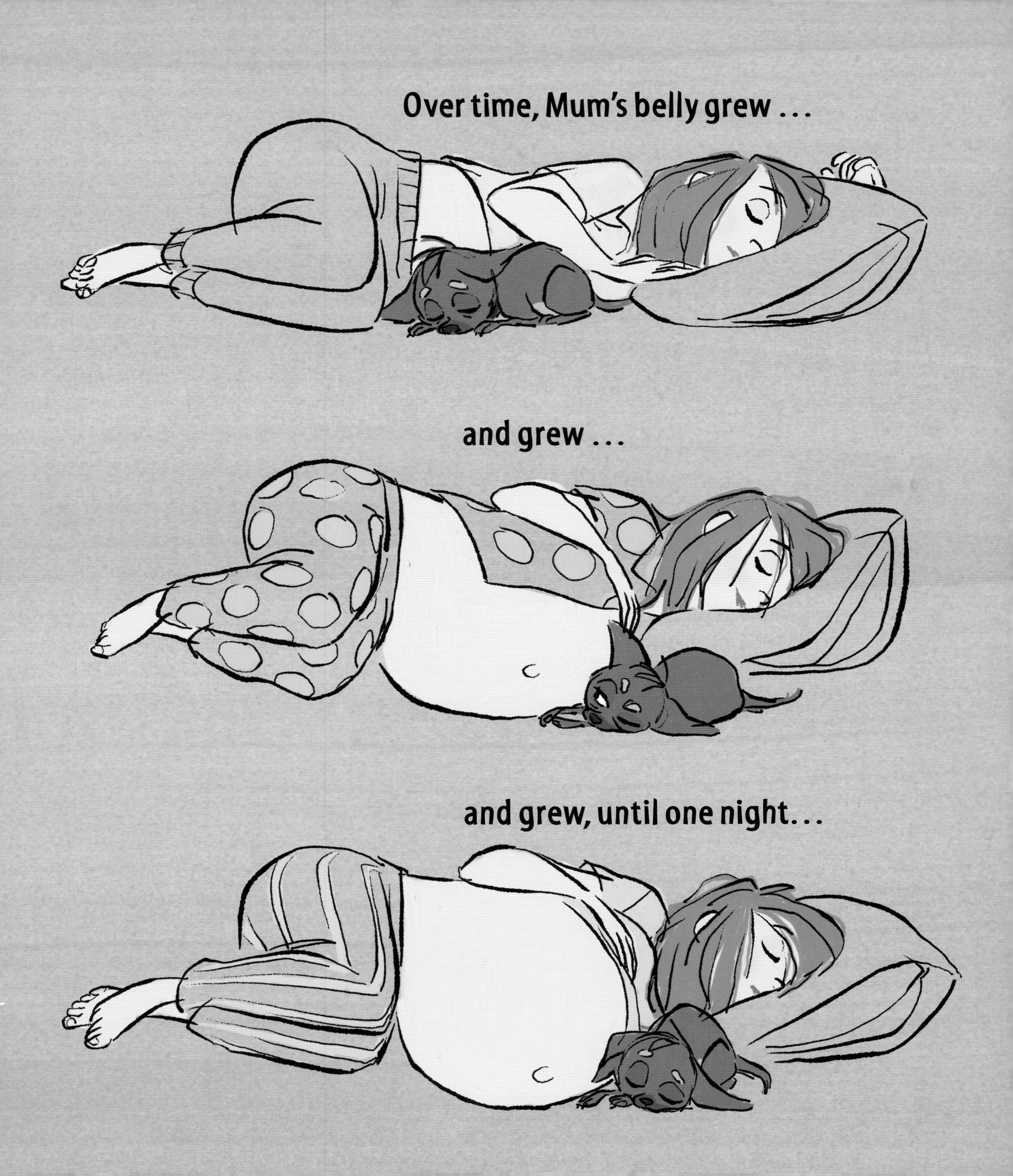
Over time, Mum's belly grew ...
and grew ...
and grew, until one night...

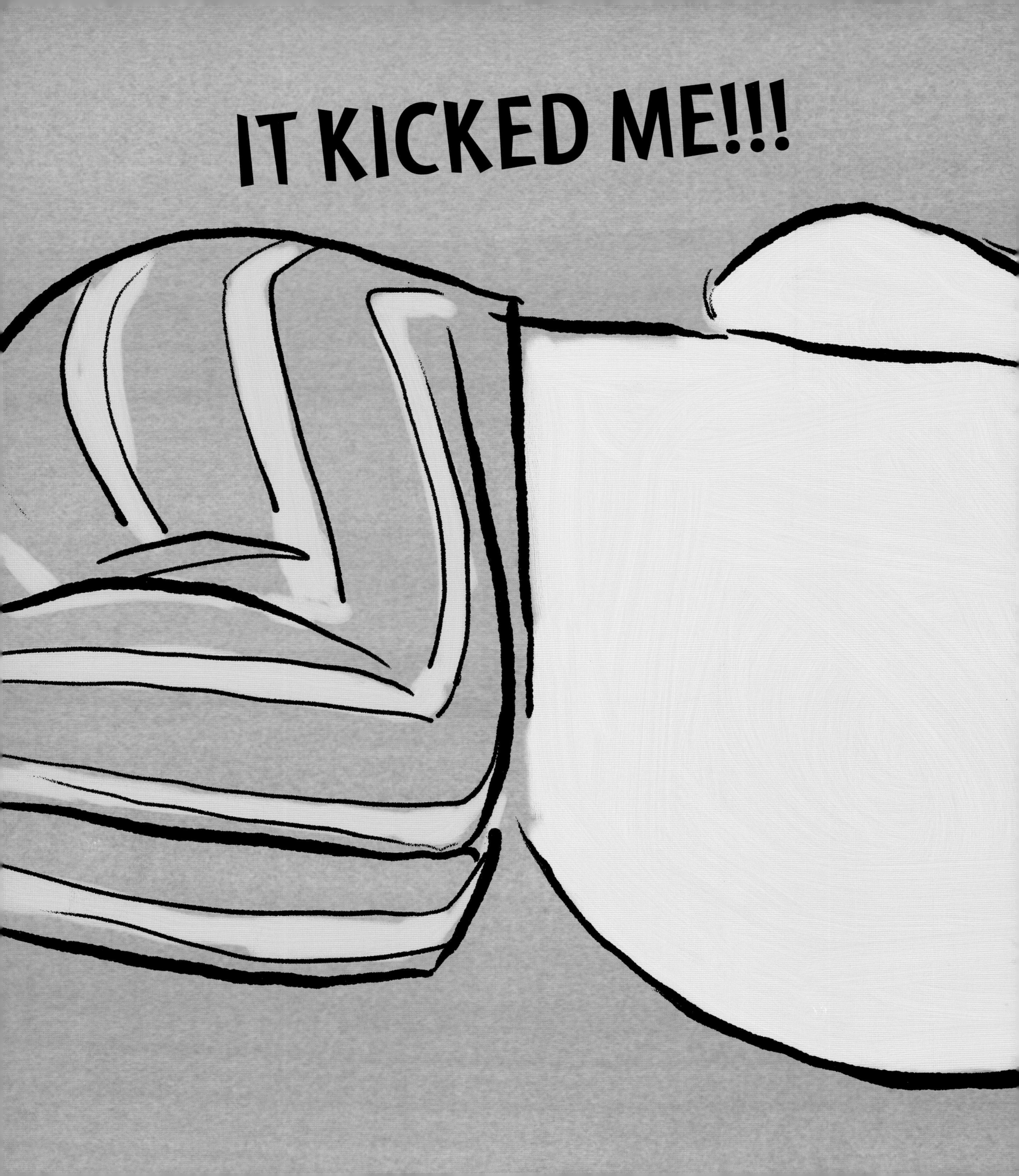

IT KICKED ME!!!

BOOMP!

From that night on, I slept on the floor.
Just me and my food bowl.
Things couldn't possibly get worse, right?

WRONG!

One day, Mum and Dad came home with lots of new stuff. At first it seemed OK.

There were two beds. Fun.

Two carriers.
Good, can't have enough of those.

Two jumpers. Cute.

Two hats. OK.
But...

Wait a minute, I thought.

What's THAT thing?

Two seats?

And that's when it hit me.

Poor Louie!

One of those creatures I could handle.
But two? No way.

Then Mum and Dad just rushed off and left me all alone. Not even a kiss goodbye!

Well, that was the last straw. I got all of my things together and ran away. For ever.

The coast was clear.

I was on my way, when . . .

"Louie, now how did you get out?"

"I must have left the door open.
Your mum and dad will be home soon.
Back you go!"

And that's it. . . The end.
My life is over.
You can close the book now. Thanks for listening.

"Lou?"

"Louie, meet your baby brother."

My baby brother...

MY BABY BROTHER!

"Poor Louie."